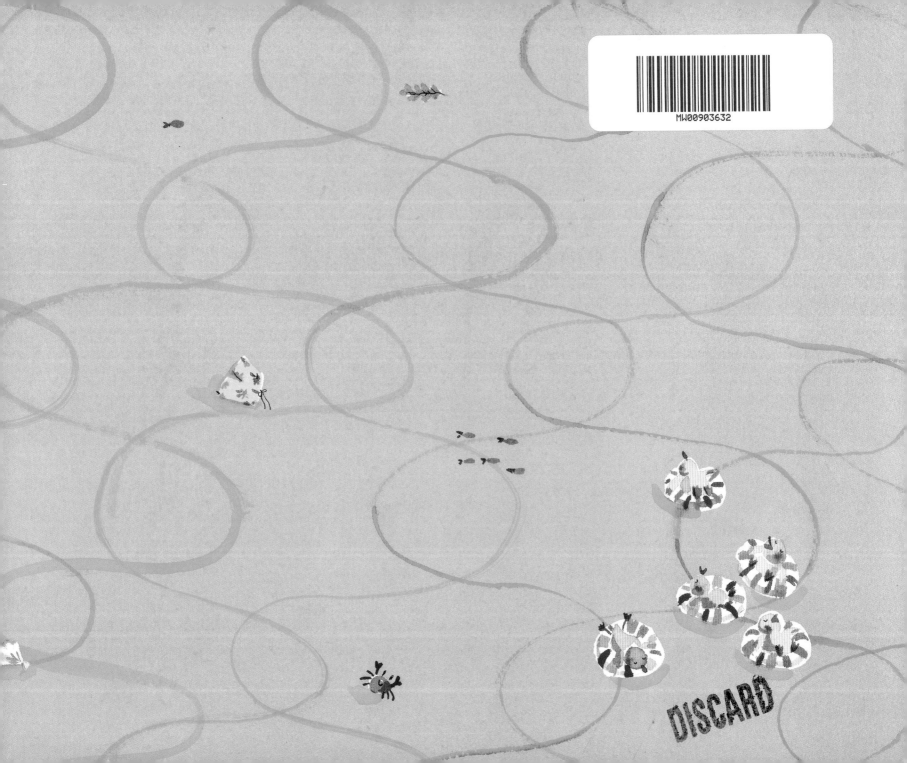

For Hiroe, Reka, and Robin—L. B.

For Koharu—H. N.

Henry Holt and Company, LLC, *Publishers since 1866*
175 Fifth Avenue, New York, New York 10010
www.HenryHoltKids.com

Henry Holt® is a registered trademark of Henry Holt and Company, LLC.
Text copyright © 2008 by Lynne Berry. Illustrations copyright © 2008 by Hiroe Nakata.
All rights reserved. Distributed in Canada by H. B. Fenn and Company Ltd.

Library of Congress Cataloging-in-Publication Data
Berry, Lynne.
Duck dunks / Lynne Berry ; illustrated by Hiroe Nakata.—1st ed.
p.   cm.
Summary: The reader is invited to count the ducks as they enjoy a day at the beach.
ISBN-13: 978-0-8050-8128-2 / ISBN-10: 0-8050-8128-3
[1. Ducks—Fiction. 2. Beaches—Fiction. 3. Counting. 4. Stories in rhyme.] I. Nakata, Hiroe, ill. II. Title.
PZ8.3.B4593Dp 2008   [E]—dc22   2007002832

First Edition—2008
The artist used watercolor and ink to create the illustrations for this book.
Printed in China on acid-free paper. ∞
1 3 5 7 9 10 8 6 4 2

Duck Dunks

Lynne Berry

ILLUSTRATED BY Hiroe Nakata

HENRY HOLT AND COMPANY ✳ NEW YORK

Ducks in swimsuits. One with a float.
One with a kite and cakes in a tote.
Five with towels—one towel each!
Five little ducks on their way to the beach.

Five little ducklings, hand in hand,

Skip from the boardwalk, into the sand.

Into the sand and into the sun—
Five little ducks see surf and run.

Ducks hit the shoreline. Ducks dive in.

Five little ducklings bob and spin.

Bobbing, splashing, ducks swim out.
Waves come crashing. Five ducks shout.

One duck gurgles.

Two ducks whirl.

Three ducks burble.

Four ducks swirl.

Five little ducks dunk undersea.

Ducks paddle up now—
"Look at me!"

Soon ducks shiver. Time for sun!

Ducks reach dry land, one by one.

towels unpack lunch:
...kes, jam cakes. Five ducks munch.

One last nibble, one last bite,

One little duck cries, "Grab that kite!"

Three hold the kite and two hold the string.

"Run, run, run, ducks!" all five sing.

Three ducks point.
Four look up high.

Five little ducks cheer, "Fly, Kite, fly!"

Ducks play leapfrog.

Ducks play tag.

"Not it! Not it!" four ducks brag.

Four ducks spy one bright red crab.

Three ducks shout. Two ducks grab.

Snippety-snap! Quick claws pinch.
Two ducks yelp. Three ducks flinch.

Five ducks watch as the sun sinks low.

"Time for a last duck-dunk. Let's go!"

Ducks towel dry and brush off sand.

Ducks waddle home now, hand in hand.

Swimsuits dripping next to a float.
Kite on a line and crumbs in a tote.

Five damp towels—one towel heap!
Five little ducks drift off to sleep.

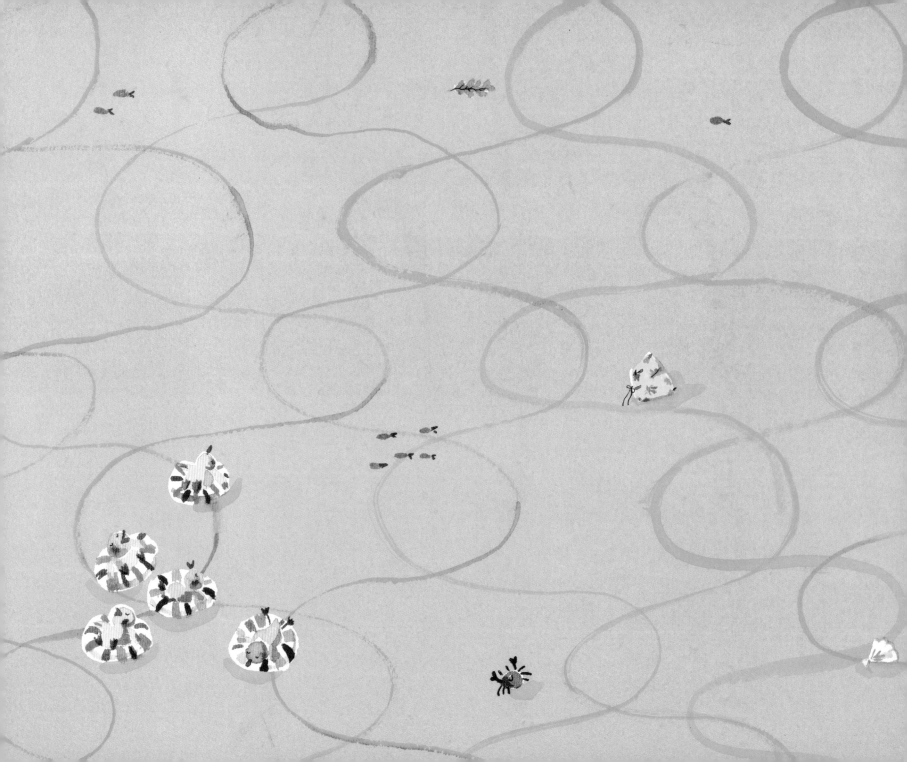